Down by the Station

illustrated by Jess Stockham

Child's Play (International) Ltd

Swindon   Auburn ME   Sydney

© A. Twinn 2002   This edition 2002   Printed in China

ISBN 0-85953-132-5

5 7 9 10 8 6

Down by the station,
Early in the morning,
See the little puffer trains
All in a row.
See the engine driver
Pull the little handle;
CHUFF! CHUFF! CHUFF!
And off we go!

chuff   chuff   chuff

Down by the station,
Early in the morning,
See the busy buses
All in a row.
See the bus driver
Calling to the passengers;
BRRM! BRRM! BRRM!
And off we go!

brrm

br

chug chug chug

Down by the station,
Early in the morning,
See the muddy tractors
All in a row.
See the tractor driver
Loading up the trailer;
CHUG! CHUG! CHUG!
And off we go!

Down by the station,
Early in the morning,
See the shiny taxi cabs
All in a row.
See the taxi driver
Polishing the windows;
BEEP! BEEP! BEEP!
And off we go!

beep   beep
    beep

honk

ho

Down by the station,
Early in the morning,
See the great big trucks
All in a row.
See the truck driver
Loading up the parcels;
HONK! HONK! HONK!
And off we go!

Down by the station,
Early in the morning,
See the fire engines
All in a row.
See the fire fighter
Climbing up the ladder;
NEE NOR! NEE NOR!
And off we go!

nee nor
nee nor
nee nor